I0540112

To those of you who jumped aboard this roller coaster with me, for listening and encouraging me, I would like to say a heart felt thank you! You all know who you are.
To my wonderful hubby and enchanting children, thank you for inspiring me and helping me to realise my dreams.
I love you all lots.

CS

In dedication to the hours spent listening, understanding,
tolerating, encouraging and the necessary propping up from my family and friends...
I say thank you x
And especially to my patient husband, loving daughter and ever kissable son...
I love you x

HH

Published by Blackbird Press 2013

Text copyright © Cassie Stafford 2013
Illustrations copyright © Harriet Hue 2013

The right of Cassie Stafford and Harriet Hue to be identified as the Author and Illustrator of this work has been asserted by them in accordance with the Copyright, Designs and Patents Act, 1988.

All rights reserved. No part of this publication may be reproduced stored or transmitted in any form, or by any means without permission from the Author and Illustrator. Any person that does any unauthorised act may be liable to criminal prosecution and civil claims for damages.

Printed in England

ISBN 978-0-9576857-0-3

www.cassieastafford.com
www.harriethue.co.uk

TWIZZLE BROWN AND LENNY SPARKLE

The Enchanted Forest

Written by Cassie Stafford

Illustrated by Harriet Hue

All was quiet, all was still
In the autumn forest over the hill.

Then a whizzing and fizzing was heard nearby
As a bright light shone out of the velvety sky.
With a BANG and a POP a wizard appeared
With a very tall hat and long silvery beard.

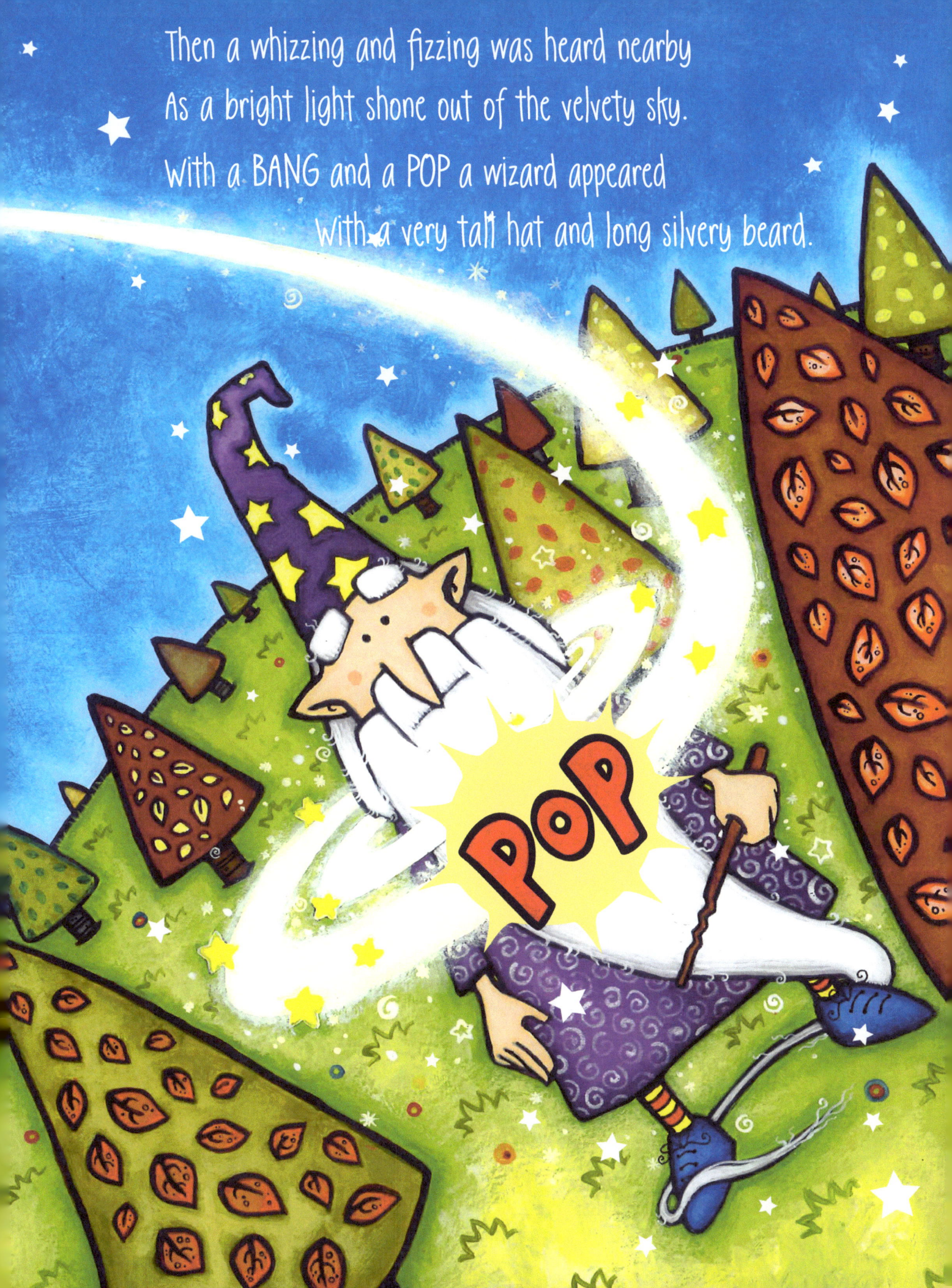

He put on his glasses and brushed down his cloak,
He picked up his satchel and then he spoke.

"Where am I?" he wondered,
"I'm not really sure.
I don't think I've ever been here before.

I'm feeling rather hungry. It's time to have a break..." With a flick of his wand he conjured his favourite food – a custard cake.

And while he
ate his custard cake,
he looked up at
the moon.
"I'm tired," he said,
"It's time for bed,
the sun will be up soon."

He laid his head
upon a bed
of earthy moss and leaves.
He put his wand
inside his cloak,
to hide from forest thieves.

But as he slept
he tossed and turned,
his wand fell to the ground.

Sparks flew out
into the night
and enchanted all they found.

A pile of autumn sticks and leaves spiralled in the air.
In the centre stood a stick man with a twizzle tuft of hair...

And a leafy little creature with big red sparkly feet.
The strangest pair of creatures you could ever hope to meet.

They gazed upon the wizard as he quietly slept.

Then
hand in hand,
into the magical forest they crept.

They looked at all the other things
the magic wand had made.
Shuffling through
the autumn leaves
they jumped and
danced and
played.

A squirrel stood and sang aloud
the most enchanting song.
A mole popped up from underground
and asked "What's going on?"

A rabbit thumped her foot and laughed,
she thought it was a joke
When she saw the frog that danced
and pranced
and curtsied
with a croak.

"Ha Ha"

A tree trunk and an owl talked late into the night.
When suddenly they jumped, they'd all received a little fright.

The Wizard appeared before them.
Confused, he scratched his head.
"I think my wand has had
a little fun tonight," he said.

"My name is Elvin, I'm a wizard.
Would you like some tea?"
He magicked a toadstool and some stools.
"So, what shall it be?

How about some cake,
some butter and some bread?
Squirrel, more nuts for you?"
"Yes please!" Squirrel said.

The Wizard sat with his new friends
who all had cake and tea.
He named each one,
and then he saw two hiding by a tree.

The Wizard was a smart one
and soon he saw them peek –
He sent his new friends Ruby Rabbit
and Felicity Frog to seek.

The Wizard beckoned the peeping pair
and asked them if they could
Take care of every creature,
big and small, inside the wood.

The two new friends smiled shyly
and bowed their heads politely
While the wizard stood above them,
with his wand, which now shone brightly.

"What shall I name you?" he pondered...
"Hmmm, now let me think..."
The wand started to sparkle,
did a jig,
and began to blink.

Into the night
shot a bright white light,
it whooshed and
popped and whizzed.

The twizzle tuft
twirled wildly,
the creature's feet
glowed then fizzed.

"I name thee Sir Lenny Sparkle,
I name thee Sir Twizzle Brown."

Rising behind them, the sun was creating
a glorious golden crown.

"From this day forth," the Wizard boomed,
"each of you will know
When a mystery needs solving, for Lenny's feet will glow.

The twizzle tuft will spin around when something is askew,
And when you are together you will know what you must do."

The forest cheered, the wizard smiled and looked up at the sun.
"It's a pleasure to have met you all, I've had a lot of fun."

He reached his hand down to the ground, but there he could not see
His satchel or his magic wand!   He cried, "Where can they be?"

The twizzle tuft twirled round and Lenny's feet began to glow.

"We can find it!" yelled Lenny Sparkle,
"Come on, Twizzle, let's go!"

They glided magically, until
Twizzle Brown said "Look!"
They found the satchel hiding in
a shady little nook.

"Thank you, Lenny, thank you, Twizzle!" the grateful wizard cried

As he took the satchel from them, with the magical wand inside.

"I hope to see you all again
but for now, I say farewell."
He swished his wand back and forth
as he muttered a magical spell.

And then he disappeared into the early morning light.
He left behind a triangle of sparkles, brilliantly white.

Will Twizzle Brown and Lenny Sparkle see their friend once more?
With all the magic in the forest, who knows what's in store?

www.ingramcontent.com/pod-product-compliance
Lightning Source LLC
Chambersburg PA
CBHW041004170626
46815CB00002B/161